Disclaimer:

All Rights Reserved. No part of this book may be reproduced or transmitted in any form or by any means, such as electronic, mechanical photocopying, recording, or otherwise, without the author's and publisher's prior written permission.

The author, copyright holder, and publisher have no responsibility for any damage or loss caused, or allegedly caused, directly or indirectly by using the information in this book.

The author, copyright holder, and publisher specifically disclaim any and all liability incurred from the use or application of the contents of this book. The information in this book is provided for entertainment purposes only and is not a substitute for professional or medical advice.

The author, copyright holder, editor, and publisher make no legal claims, express or implied. The contents are not intended to replace the services of a qualified physician or professional.

Paperback edition.

Copyright 2024. Global Enterprises and Holdings Inc., 2024

All Rights Reserved. Paperback Edition ISBN ISBN: 978-1-7334831-8-6

Published by Global Enterprises and Holdings Inc., 2024.

smurrell@geholdingsinc.com

In a land where eagles soar, Independence Day we do adore.
The children cheer at the sky so bright.
The colossal flag is a dazzling sight as fireworks burst in the night.

Independence Day we do adore.

Independence Day we do adore.

Independence Day we do adore.

Independence Day we do adore.

Long ago, in the days of yore, patriots fought for something more. Their courage was a resounding roar. Thirteen colonies, hearts aflame, to break from tyranny was their aim.

Patriots fought for something more.

Patriots fought for something more.

Patriots fought for something more.

Patriots fought for something more.

The leader, George Washington, was so bold.
He guided patriots, their story forever told.
Through battles fought day and night
for freedom's cause, they stood to fight.

George Washington was so bold.

George Washington was so bold.

16

With quills in hand, the Founders wrote a declaration with hope afloat.
A nation's birth is a moment to denote.
In Philadelphia, on parchment fair, they declared independence, a daring affair.

A nation's birth is a moment to denote.

A nation's birth is a moment to denote.

A nation's birth is a moment to denote.

A nation's birth is a moment to denote.

A nation's birth is a moment to denote.

A nation's birth is a moment to denote.

The Liberty Bell's sound rings.
The bell of freedom sings!
To a chorus of liberty, the bell clings.
Across the land, its echoes resound; in our hearts, freedom is found.

The Liberty Bell's sound rings.

July 4th, 1776, was the United States of America's decree. To celebrate, we dance with glee. It's Independence Day, and we are free!

July 4th, 1776, was America's decree.

July 4th, 1776, was America's decree.

July 4th, 1776, was America's decree.

July 4th, 1776, was America's decree.

We cherish this land so free,
from the mountains to the sea.
With fireworks bright and bonfires tall,
we parade through each city, town, and hall.

We parade through each city.

We parade through each city.

We parade through each city.

We parade through each city.

Families gather with friends in tow.
We celebrate with sparklers that glow.
Together, our spirits grow.
With gatherings and laughter sweet, in our hearts, freedom's beat.

We celebrate with sparklers that glow.

We celebrate with sparklers that glow.

We celebrate with sparklers that glow.

We celebrate with sparklers that glow.

From fields of green to oceans wide,
we honor those who fought and died.
With gratitude, our hearts abide.
For liberty's sake, they stood tall;
their sacrifice, we recall.

With gratitude, our hearts abide.

With gratitude, our hearts abide.

With gratitude, our hearts abide.

With gratitude, our hearts abide.

40

Tales of heroes, past and new, stars and stripes, red, white, and blue. With joy and reverence, we celebrate our nation, which is strong and great.

With joy, we celebrate our nation.

With joy, we celebrate our nation.

With joy, we celebrate our nation.

With joy, we celebrate our nation.

So let's rejoice,
both young and
old,
in the stories of
freedom told.
In unity, our spirits
unfold.
On Independence
Day, let's stand
for the ideals of
this great land.

In unity, our spirits unfold.

Questions

1) Why do we celebrate Independence Day?

2) When do we observe Independence Day?

3) Research and write a paragraph about the Declaration of Independence.

Add Your Rhyme

Co-Author

Draw and Color

Draw and Color

Draw and Color

Draw and Color

Draw and Color

Draw and Color

Draw and Color

Draw and Color

Draw and Color

Draw and Color

Draw and Color

Draw and Color

Draw and Color

Draw and Color

Draw and Color